Buster Catches a Wave

by Marc Brown

 LITTLE, BROWN AND COMPANY

New York ⚓ Boston

Little, Brown and Company, Time Warner Book Group

1271 Avenue of the Americas, New York, NY 10020 • www.lb-kids.com

First Edition: September 2005

Library of Congress Cataloging-in-Publication Data

Brown, Marc Tolon.

Buster catches a wave/ Marc Brown.—1st ed.   p. cm.—(Postcards from Buster)

Summary: When his father takes him to visit Florida, Buster sends postcards to his friends back home telling them what he is learning about surfing.

ISBN 0-316-15903-4 (hc)— ISBN 0-316-00122-8 (pb)

[1. Surfing—Fiction. 2. Beaches—Fiction. 3. Rabbits—Fiction. 4. Postcards—Fiction. 5. Florida—Fiction.]

I. Title. II. Series: Brown, Marc Tolon. Postcards from Buster. PZ7.B81618 Bjb2005 [E]—dc22   2004018619

Printed in the United States of America • PHX • 10 9 8 7 6 5 4 3 2 1

All photos from *Postcards from Buster* courtesy of WGBH Boston and Cinar Productions, Inc., in association with Marc Brown Studios.

Do you know what these words MEAN?

balance (BA-lens): to stay in a steady position

currents (KUR-ents): moving water set in motion by gravity, wind, and other forces

jellyfish: a sea animal that has a soft body shaped like an umbrella

riding the wave: another way to describe surfing

side fins: part of a commonly used three-fin surfboard design

surfboard: a long, flat board used to ride on top of a wave

trail fin: the center fin in the tri-fin design, resembling the fin on a dolphin's back

Cocoa Beach, Florida

- Cocoa Beach, Florida, is part of a 72-mile stretch of shoreline along the eastern coast of Florida.

- The alligator is the official state reptile of Florida.

- The sport of surfing began thousands of years ago in Polynesia. It became really popular in the 1950s.

"Buster, why are you
wearing sunglasses?"
Arthur asked.

"I'm going to the beach,"
Buster explained.
"It's good to practice."

When Buster and his father
got to Florida,
they met some surfers
named Joe and Forrest.

Dear Muffy,

Surfers wear rubber suits to keep warm in cold water. They look like tall seals.

Buster

Muffy Cross
432 Valley
Elwood C

Forrest showed Buster
the trail fin
and the side fins
on his surfboard.

"They help steady the board
in the water," he said.

Dear Binky,

On a surfboard,
you have to put your feet
in just the right places.
If you forget, you'll be sorry.

Buster

Binky Barnes
10 Pine Tree Road
Elwood

Forrest showed Buster
his surf swing.

"That's a skateboard!"
said Buster.

Forrest nodded.
"Standing on it
helps you learn balance."

Francine Frensky
Maple Drive Apt. 5
Elwood

Buster took a surfing class
and learned about
strong currents
and sharks and jellyfish.

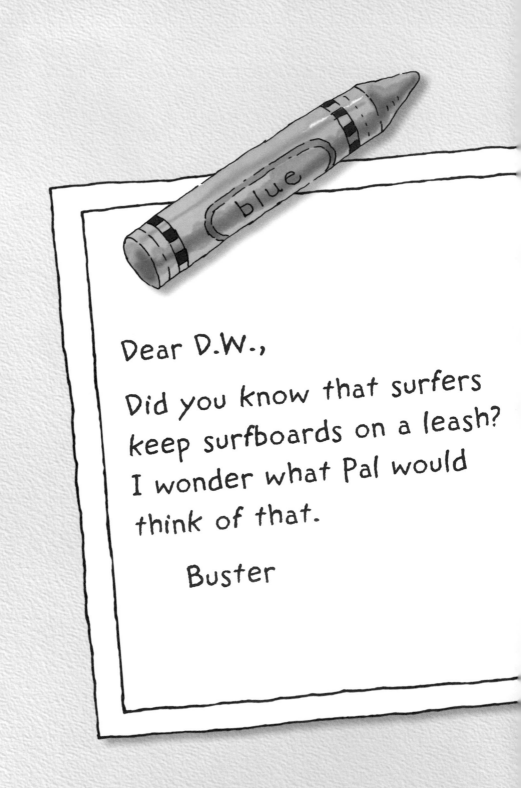

D.W. Read
100 Main Street
Elwoo

Buster even practiced
jumping on a trampoline.

Forrest showed him how to
do a front flip and a tail grab.

Dear Mom,
Joe says that a good surfer
"becomes" water.
If I become water,
I'll try not to make a mess.
Buster

Then, Buster went
surfing again.
He rode his board
through a big wave.

Dear Arthur,

The waves look a lot
bigger up close.
And they're a lot louder, too.

Buster

Arthur Read
100 Main Street
Elw

Buster caught
the next wave perfectly.

"Hey, I'm riding the wave!"
he shouted.

"Woooohoooo!"

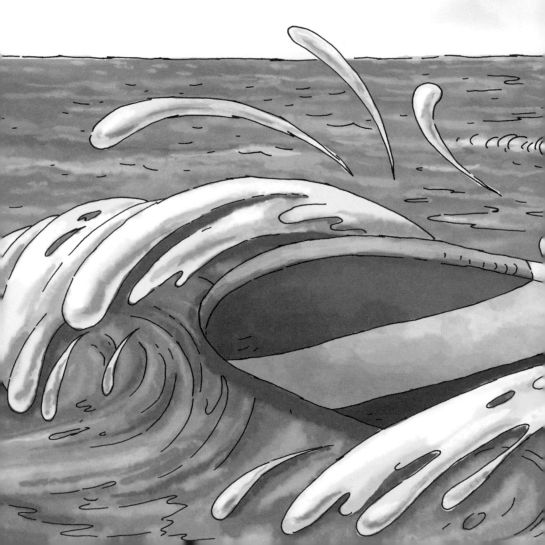

Dear Forrest and Joe,

I'm still practicing here on my skateboard.

The next time I catch a wave, I'll make sure it doesn't get away.

Buster